Please delete address not required before mailing

PHAIDON PRESS INC.
180 Varick Street
New York
NY 10014

PHAIDON PRESS LIMITED
Regent's Wharf
All Saints Street
London N1 9PA

Return address for USA and Canada only

Return address for UK and countries outside the USA and Canada only

Affix stamp here

Dear Reader, Books by Phaidon are recognised world-wide for their beauty, scholarship and elegance. We invite you to return this card with your name and e-mail address so that we can keep you informed of our new publications, special offers and events. Alternatively, visit us at **www.phaidon.com** to see our entire list of books, videos and stationery. Register on-line to be included on our regular e-newsletters.

Subjects in which I have a special interest

☐ Art ☐ Contemporary Art ☐ Architecture ☐ Design ☐ Photography

☐ Music ☐ Art Videos ☐ Fashion ☐ Decorative Arts ☐ *Please send me a complimentary catalogue*

Mr/Miss/Ms Initial Surname

Name

No./Street

City Country

Post code/Zip code

E-mail

This is not an order form. To order please contact Customer Services at the appropriate address overleaf.

sempé

Sunny Spells

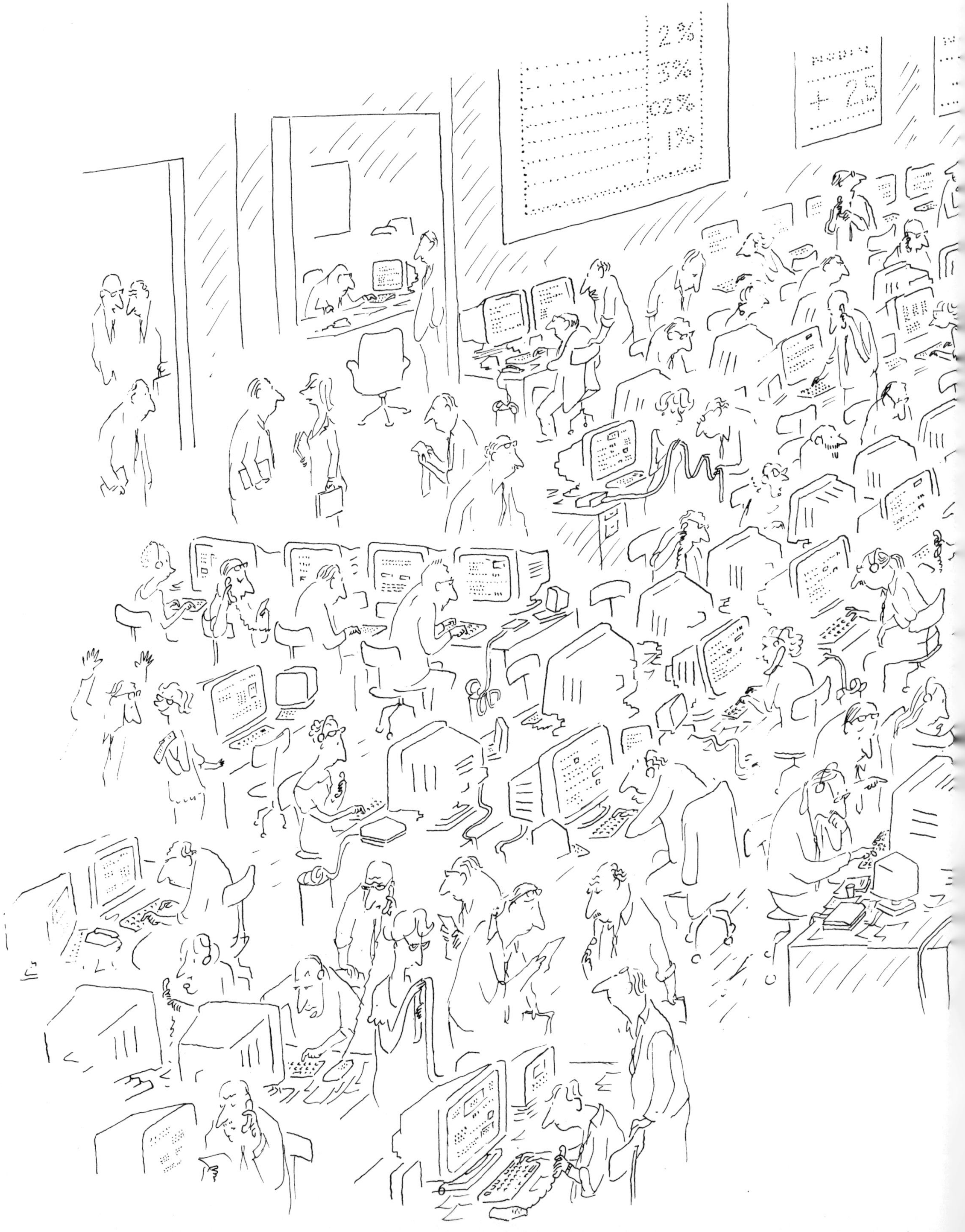
2 %
3%
02 %
1%
+ 25

Granny, I want you to dig up those old golden louis d'or coins under the fig tree. Oh, come on, Granny, I always knew they were there! There are 18 of them. Take them to the bank and tell Mr Leleu to buy yen (that's Japanese money). Then he must convert the yen into dollars tomorrow, and buy back into louis d'or coins the day after tomorrow. There'll be 21 of them. Leleu will be really surprised. Give one of the gold coins to his daughter Francine and tell her I'm thinking of her. I'd rather like to step into Leleu's job when he retires. The air is very polluted here in Paris, and you hardly ever see the sun.

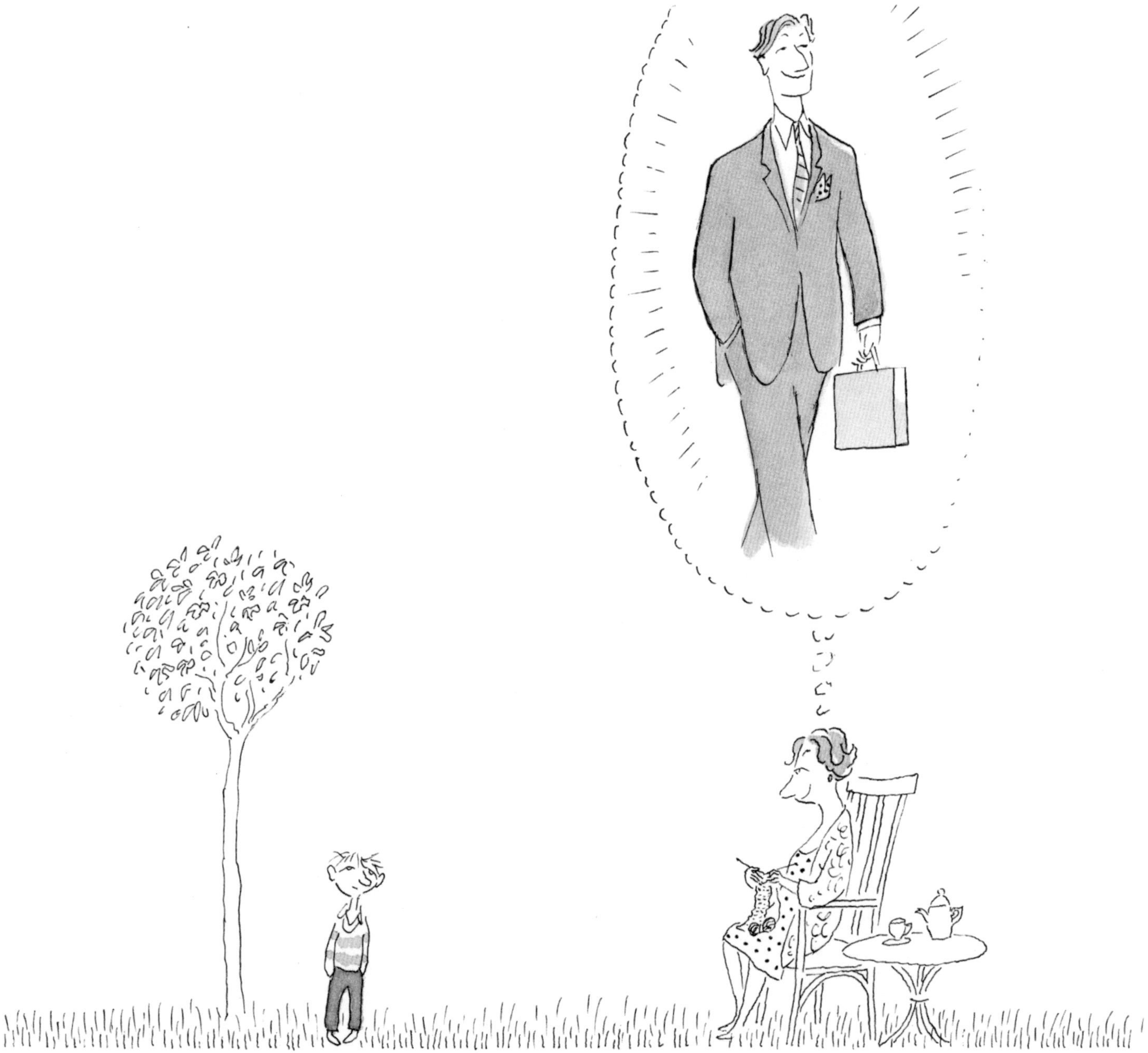

On days like this I feel invincible.

When we grow up we'll wear bathing suits, OK. But, judging by what I know of grown-ups from their movies and their TV shows, I'll have to take you out to expensive restaurants then, places where we'll eat much the same things as we're eating here, just to make you agree to take your bathing suit off one day.

After hearing the evidence and examining the files, the disciplinary committee has decided that the winner of the Prix Goncourt, having tested positive for drugs, will be downgraded to winner of the Prix Renaudot.

Of course we must make sure it doesn't become addictive, but if you take one of these capsules in the middle of the afternoon, by around six or seven in the evening you can be almost sure of feeling that slight melancholy which is an intrinsic part of human nature.

I found my bike!

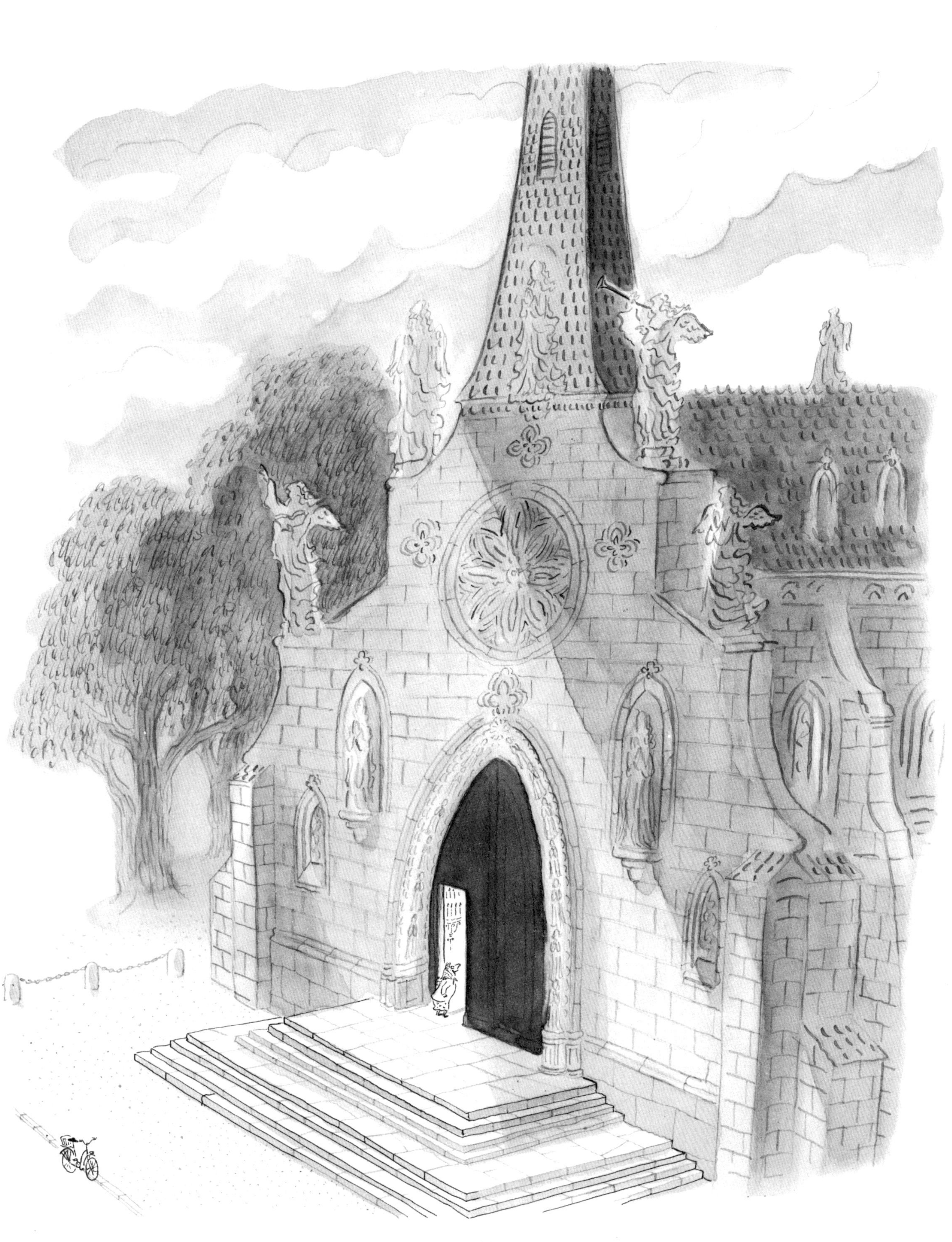

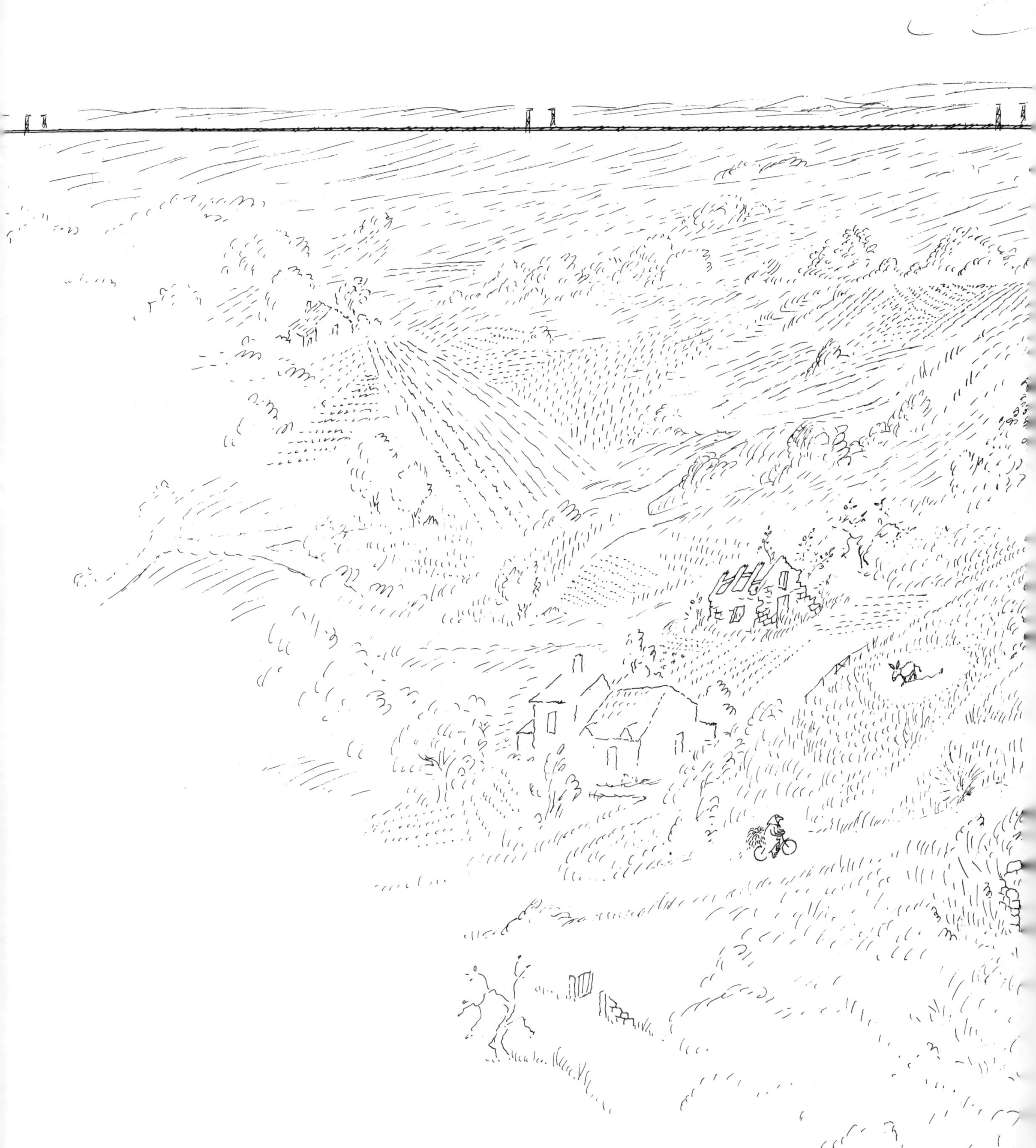

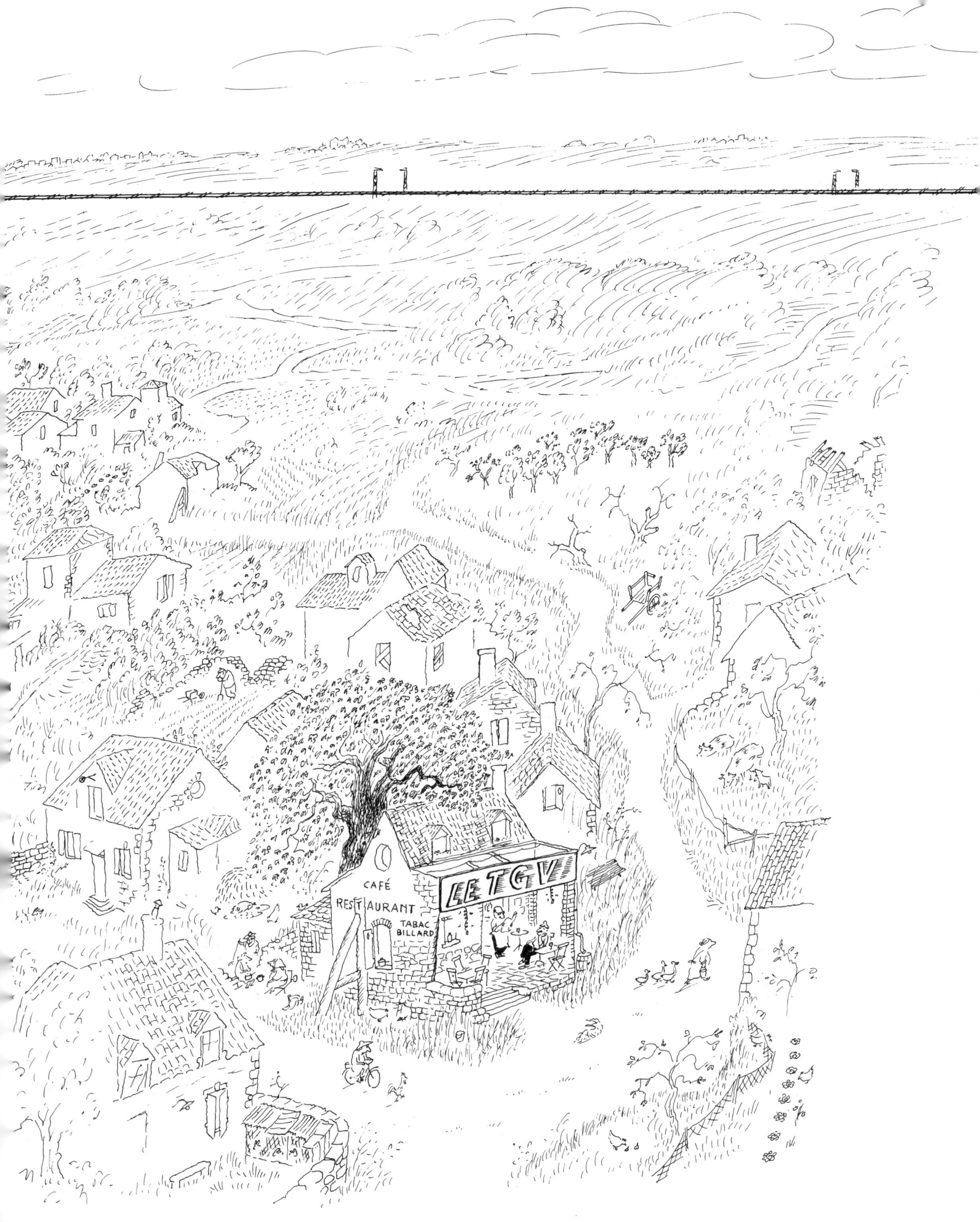
CAFÉ
RESTAURANT
TABAC
BILLARD
LE TGV

I expect you've switched off your mobile because you're in a meeting, as usual! So my voice ends up in your bag along with a whole lot of notebooks, key rings, make-up, toothbrush, spare tights, peppermints, etc. Don't you see that this is really getting me down? Let's have some real home life. It would help me a lot. Working in television is tough, you have to fight your way to the top. If my home life was different I could make it. I might even get to present the main news. And every evening, I'd make a little signal, just for you, that no one else would notice!

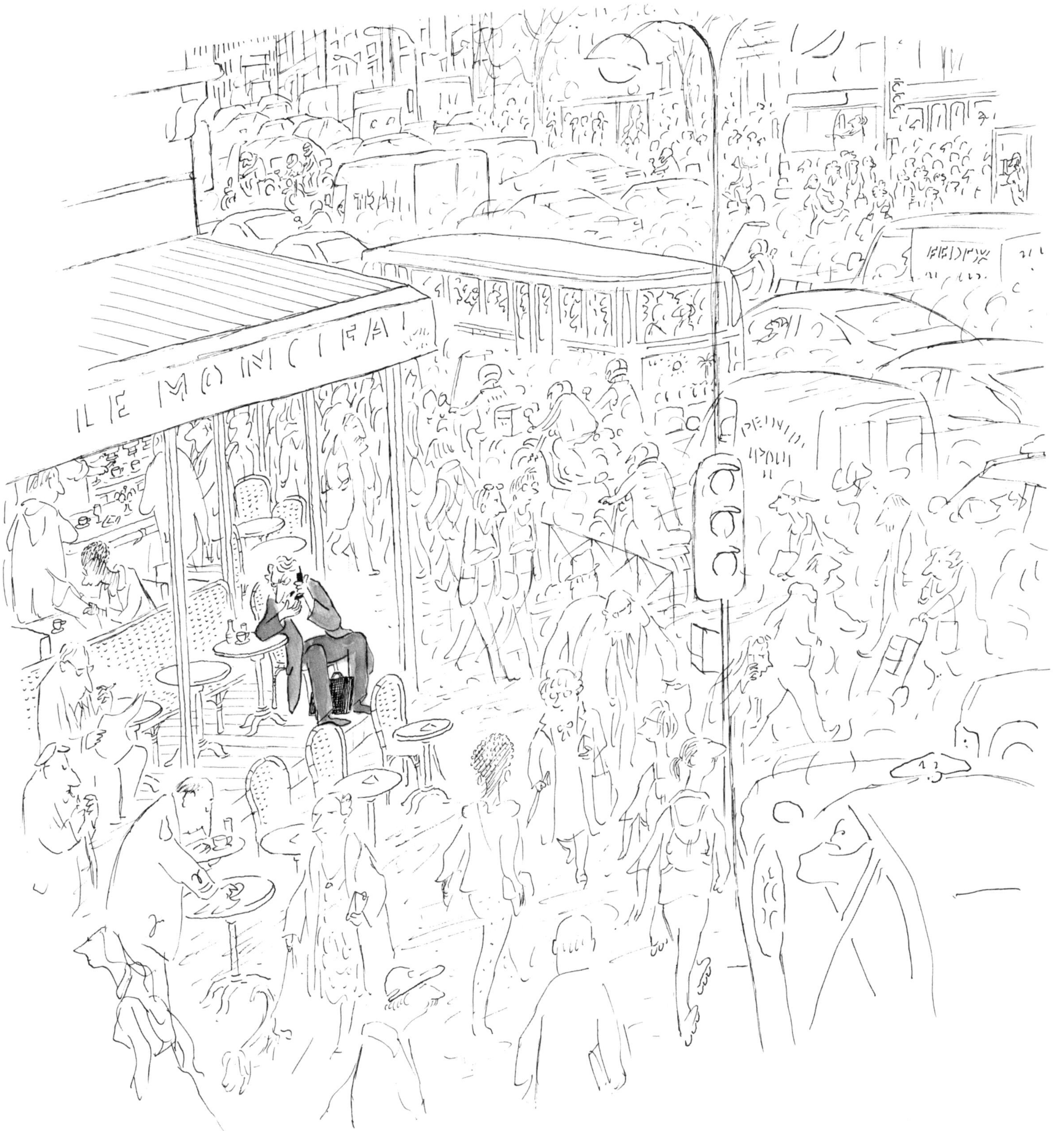

We thought it was a delightful evening too, with almost no home truths left untold.

They tell us: God is dead. So no more metaphysics. And then what's left? Mankind and Nature. That won't get you far.

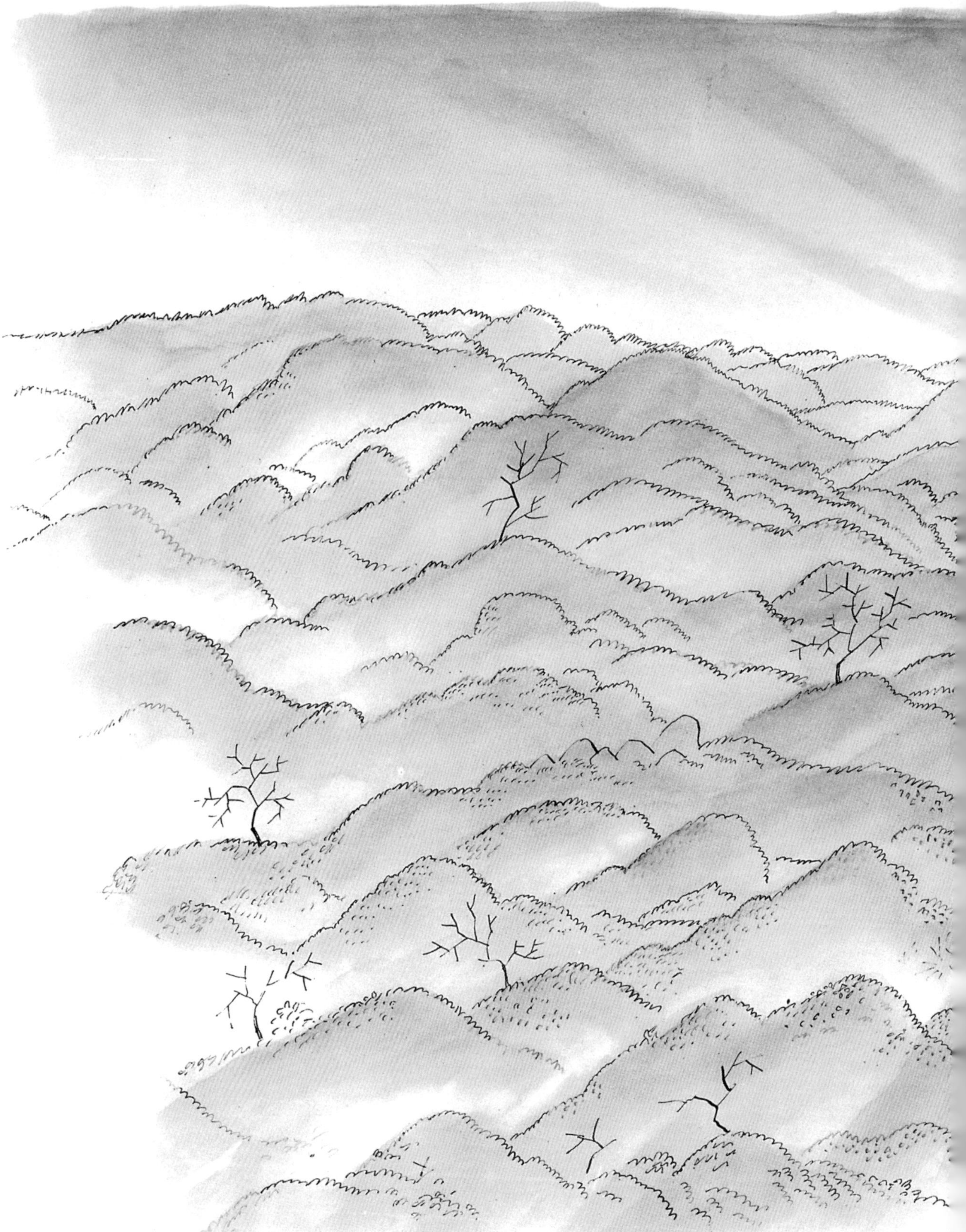

"Didn't get much sleep on account of mosquitoes. Did not feel guilty about leaving the group (I thought it would be interesting) until I found out that what I thought was a distress rocket in the bag they gave us yesterday was only a big stick of barley sugar. Will wait an hour or so and then throw the barley sugar as high in the air and as far as possible. You never know."

"Landowner, dreamer and poet, WLTM kindred spirit, with view to marriage, must have similar qualities and also be very down to earth."

"Girl who got on at Châtelet station. Big blue eyes, yellow raincoat. We clicked. A sudden jolt threw you against me. I held you very close. You were deeply moved. You suddenly got off at Hôtel-de-Ville. Keep the money and my wallet. Send me back my papers."

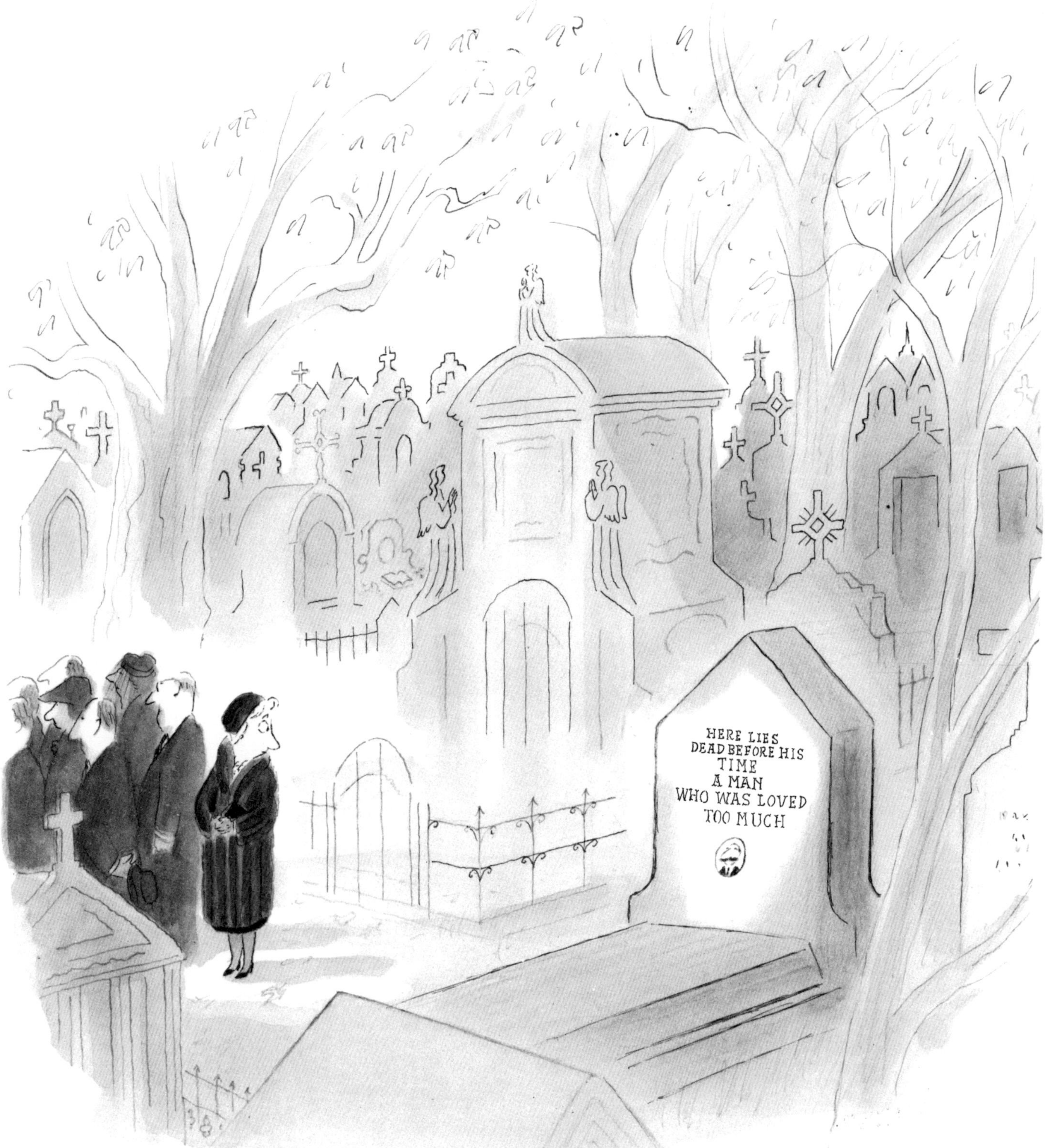
HERE LIES
DEAD BEFORE HIS
TIME
A MAN
WHO WAS LOVED
TOO MUCH

We're going to try driving into town to deliver this manuscript to my publishers. It describes, in detail, the deterioration of a relationship in which one partner is a male chauvinist pig. The book will be quite a sensation, and in the course of the TV coverage, I would like you to testify to the fact that I have been prevented from practising my profession as a writer to the very end.

We're looking for a book that hasn't been picked up by the media. A top-quality work. And if we think it's really good then we'll set off the irresistible force known as the word-of-mouth campaign.

Of course he's gay. I've never heard him say anything unkind about women.

*Look at that fly rubbing its front legs, the way you rub your hands when you're feeling happy.
What I'm writing at the moment must be really good.*

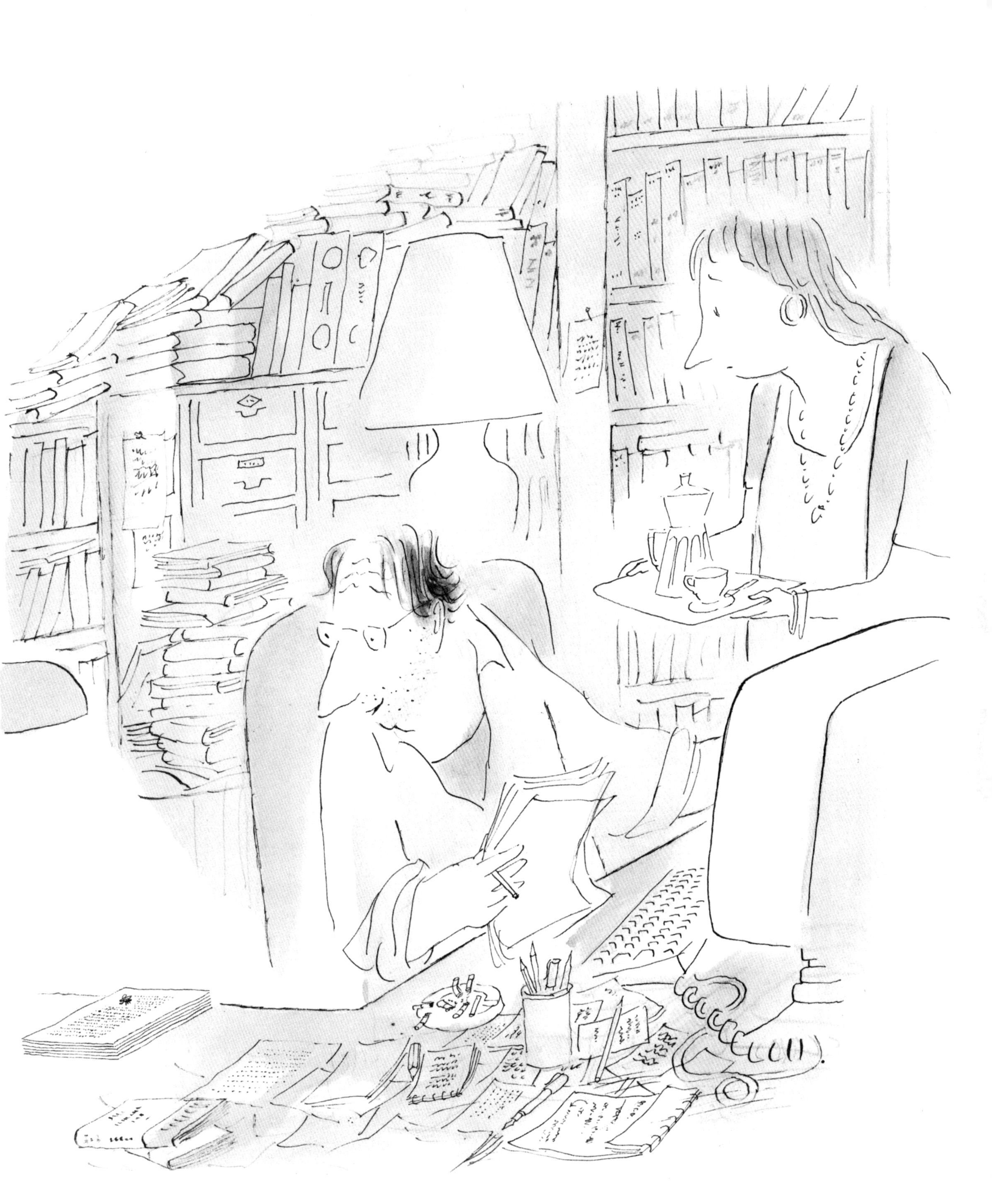

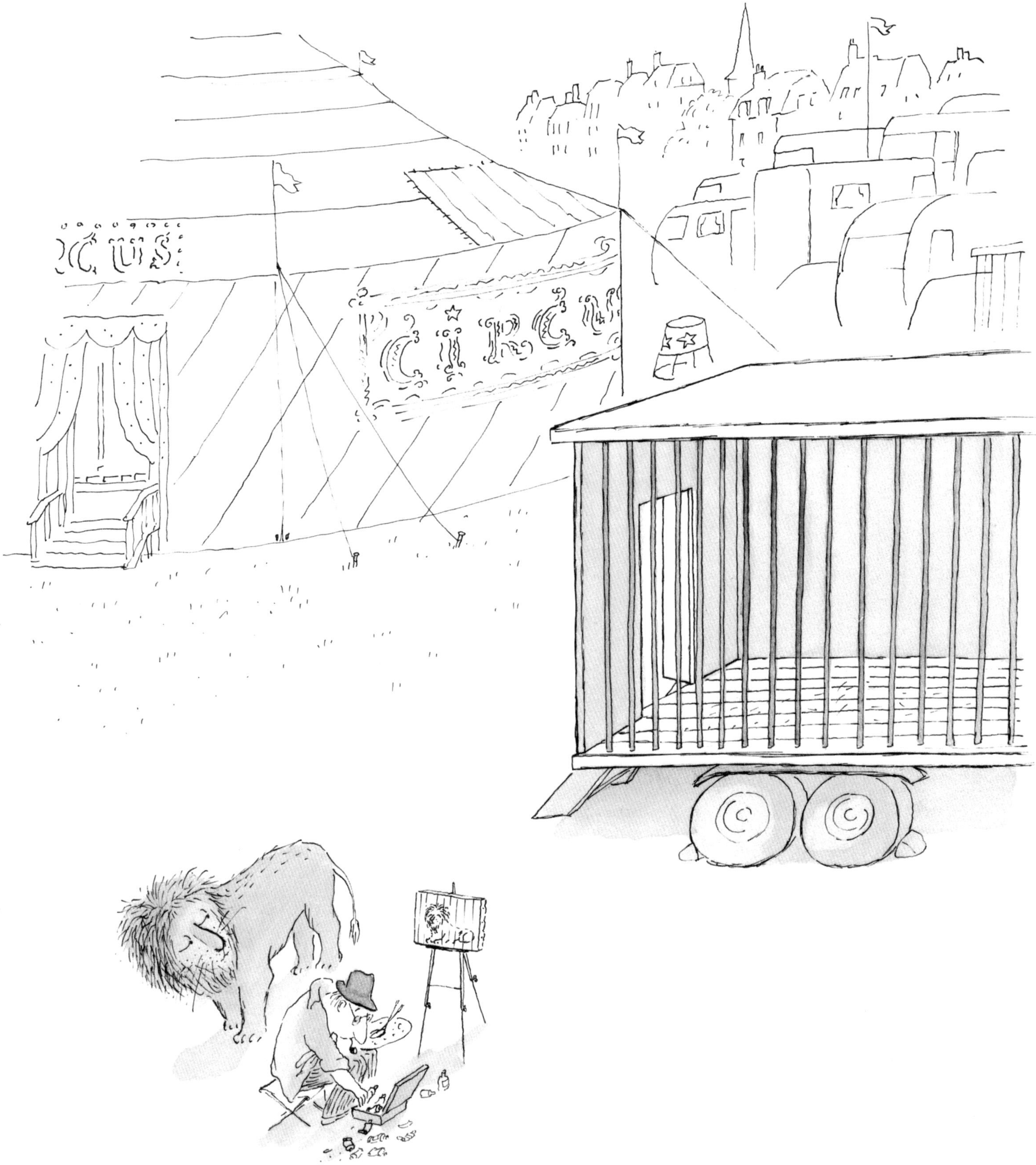

Yesterday I realized that Sophie and I have nothing in common. I was looking at my picture 'Orchard after the Storm' over the chest of drawers, and I murmured, with a touch of melancholy: "Is it always to stay like this?" And Sophie said: "We might as well leave it there for the time being."

It's not decided yet. She hasn't finished her last chapter. But from what I've read on the sly, I don't figure among Great Men She Has Known.

NO TO QUOTAS ON
BACK TO BASICS
FEDERATION
OUI!
NON!
NEGOTIATION
NO MORE TAXES ON
SUR
REFORM
2ND YEAR
NO TO THE LAW
I FEEL BAD ALL OVER
DOWN WITH THE IMPOSITION OF
SUR
TEACHERS' UNION

During dinner I felt a bond of sympathy arise between us. Here, this is my private diary. I'll call you the day after tomorrow to find out what you think of it.

And finally Howard, who was thought to be dead, will return and, after many twists and turns of the plot, will be reunited with Hélène. I shall be giving the book a happy ending, and the black veil of mourning that has covered our literature for too long will at last be lifted.

Exercise 1: classic recipe for chicken fricassee. No protests, please, we're going to work up some literary suspense. Tomorrow, Exercise 2: did he tell you to make the chicken fricassee or did you suggest it yourself? The day after tomorrow, Exercise 3: the reasons why you end up tipping the chicken fricassee over his head.

You must understand one thing: your wife's attitude is not directed against you personally. It's only an expression of historical retaliation.

And do you ever sell any?

I do hope you're writing something nice for after the summer holidays.

I read your poem last night. I could say all sorts of things about it, but we're starting for home very early tomorrow. Maybe we can discuss it next year?

"I often have this dream: I cannot name
The woman whom I love, who takes my hands.
She's never strange, yet never quite the same.
She loves me, though, and always understands."

No, not tonight, Charles. I'd rather play classical music tonight.

And now let one hell of a thrill go through you!

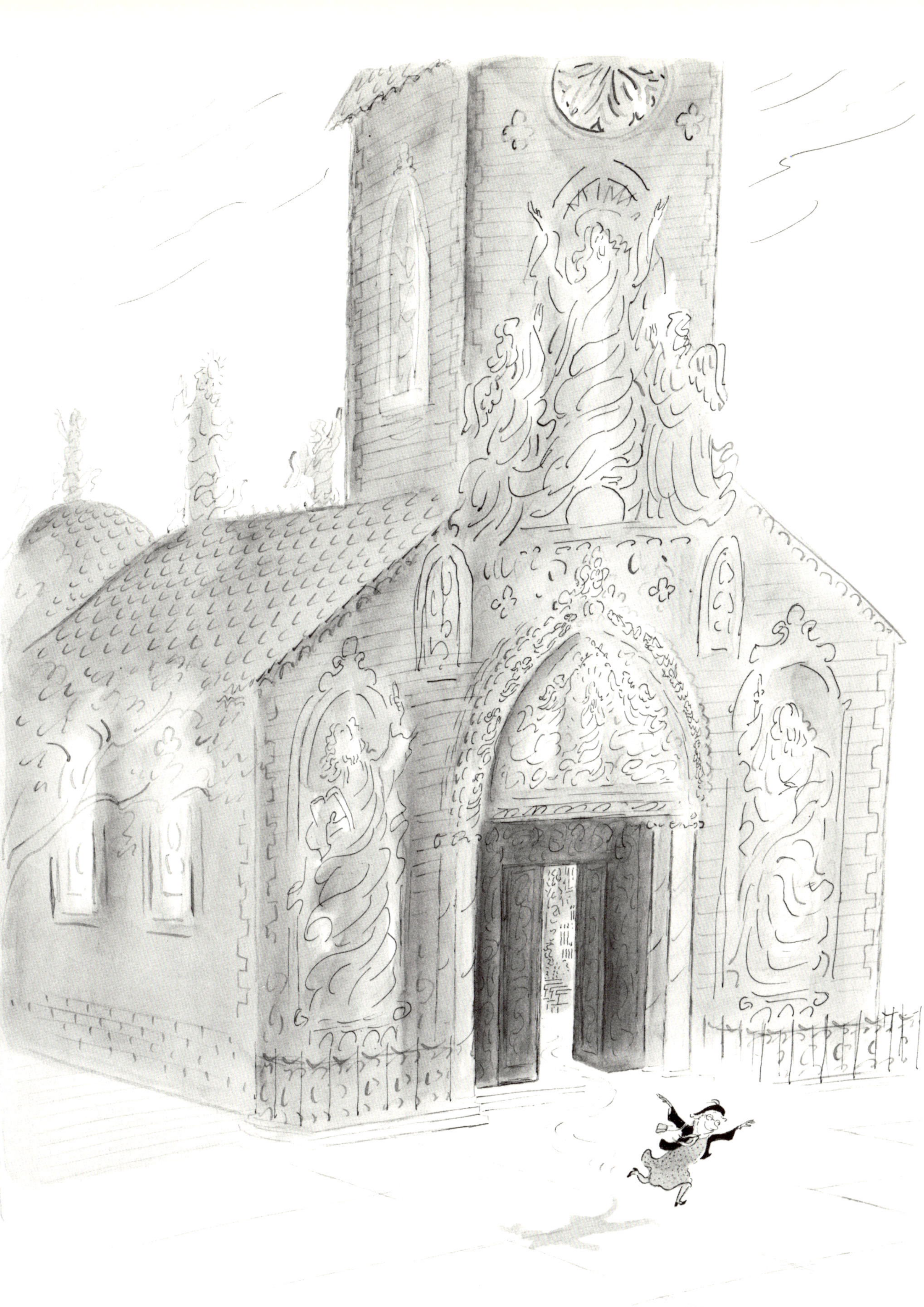

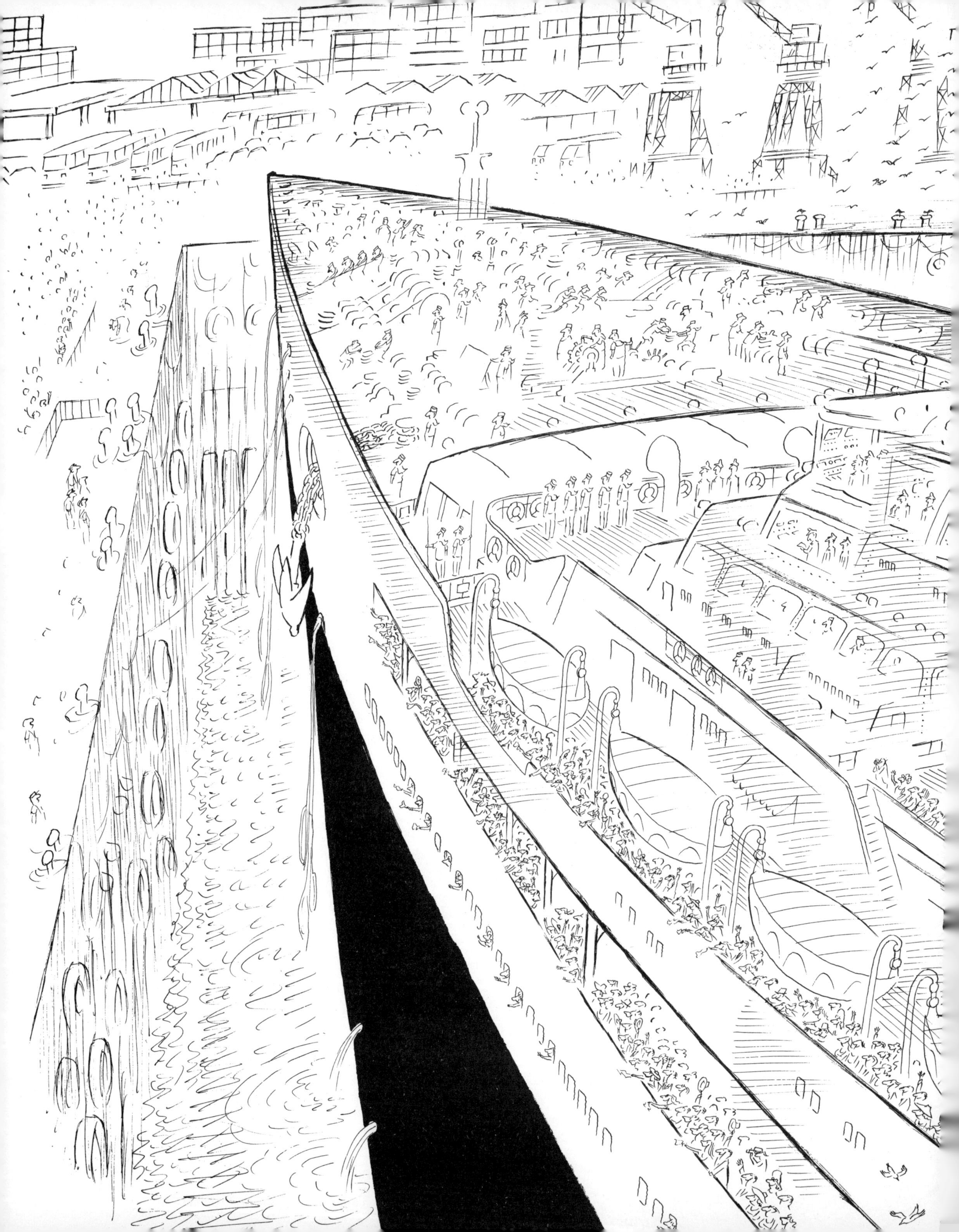

I make myself as small as I can on board ship, so as not to get in the way when the vessel's manoeuvring.

They're doing much better since she stopped talking to them.

*I talk in my sleep. Marie-Laure has told me so. It can happen to anyone, I know. But it's what I say that puzzles me.
It seems that I announce, two or three times a night: "I am completely in control."*

You'll be glad to know that he likes the idea of being half of a couple very much. You may not be so glad to know that you're not the other half.

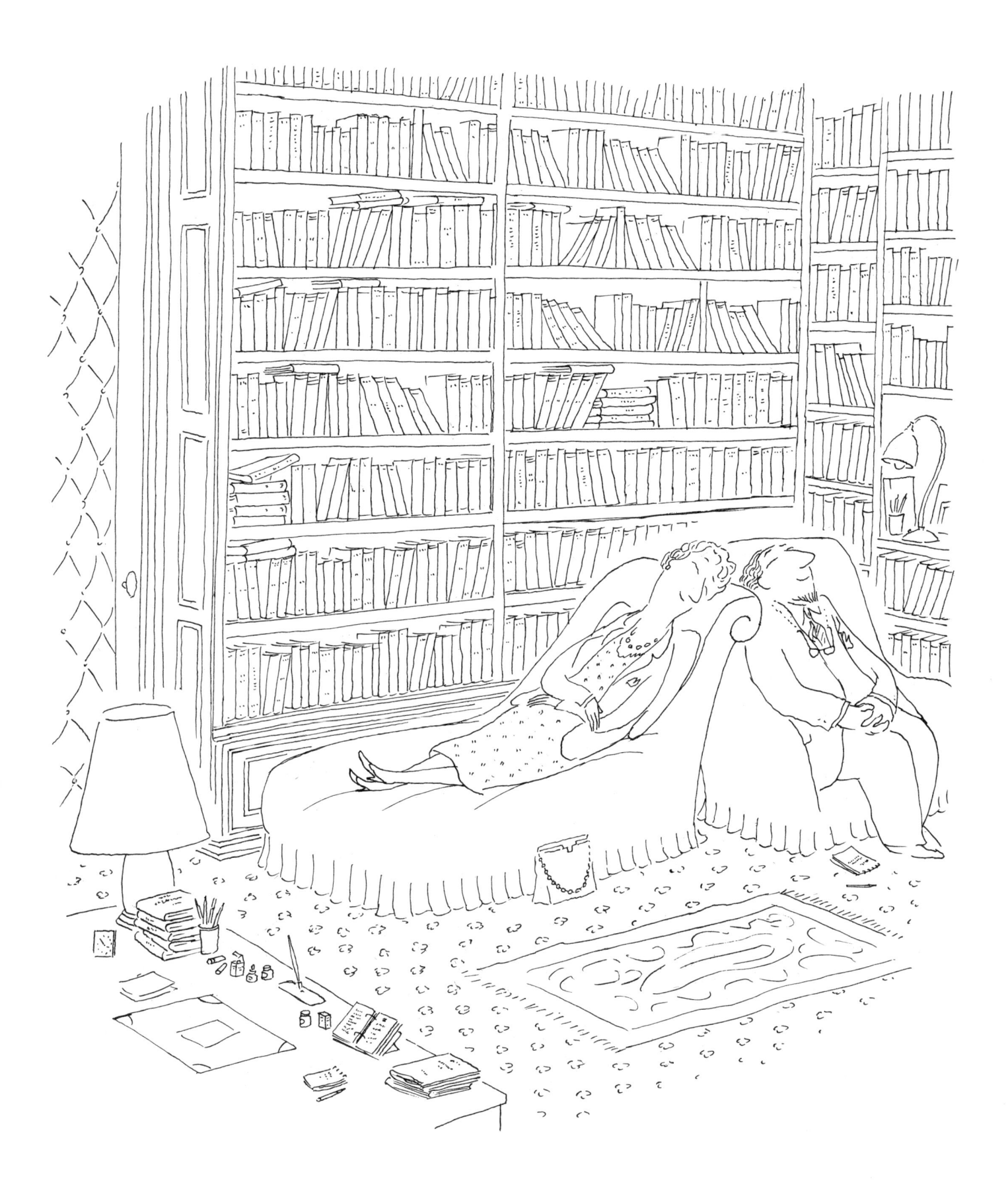

Yes, really, I've been watching her for several days: they're sweeping movements, she repeats them very slowly, and they must come in extremely useful about the house.

You really want this sofa. For the last two weeks you have been admitting that you could quietly abstract 200 euros a month from the family budget. Last week you said you could pretend that your aunt had made you a present of it. But now a deep sense of guilt prevents you from taking further action. Shall we discuss the matter calmly?

No offence meant, but did you know that when you're unhappy you're far more interesting than at times like this, when things are going well for you?

He's a good actor, but after he's said a few of his lines he just can't help mentioning his personal problems.

Do you feel it, too? When I read the words "Attack on National Security", a kind of delicious shiver runs up my spine.

Looks like I won't be seeing much of you today.

Going to see one's husband in hospital every day isn't very convenient, but on the other hand it's reassuring to know someone who's plumbing anything these days, even the depths.

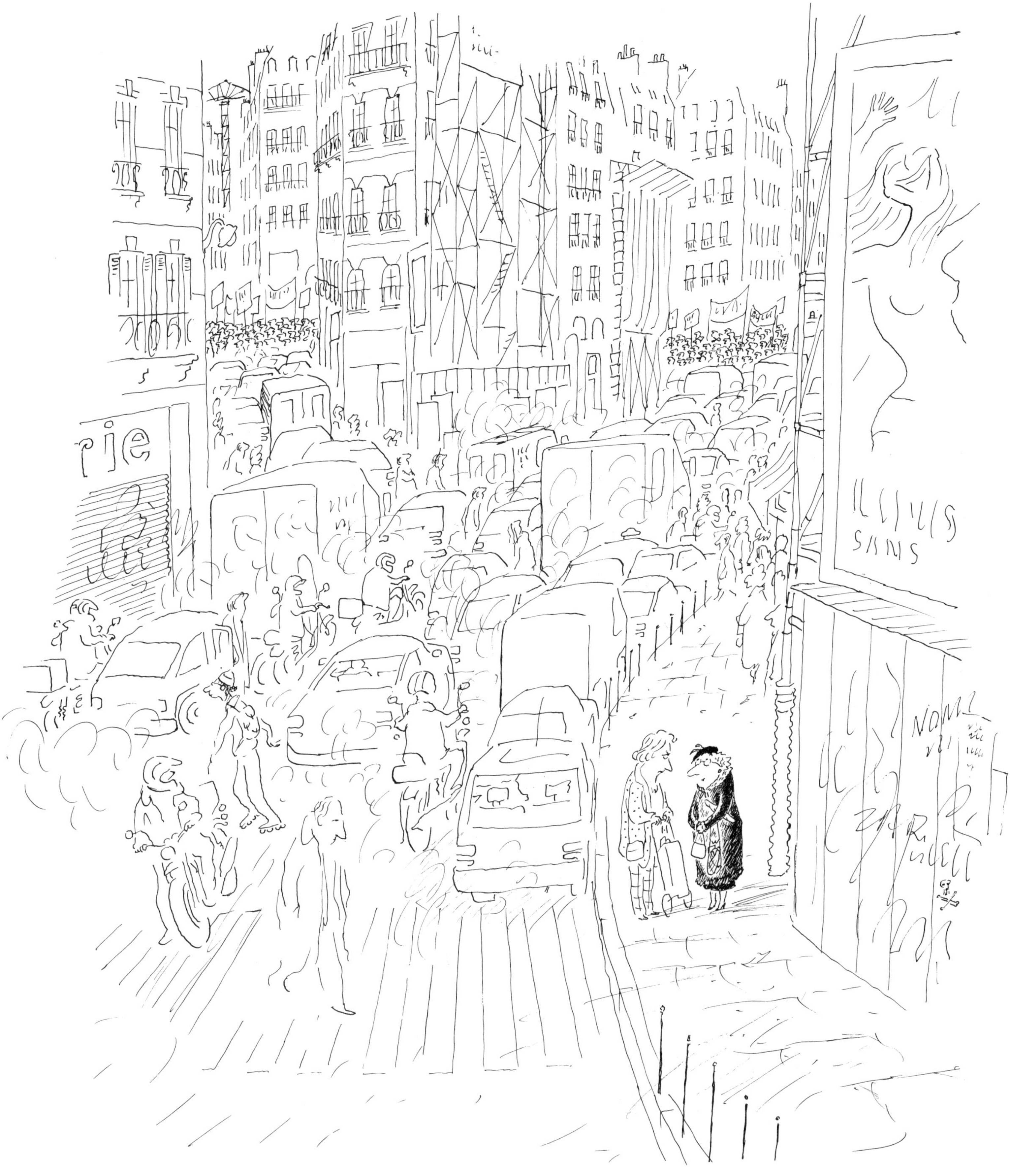
rie
SANS

It was a fine day. I was young and pretty in my wedding dress. My family and friends were all there. The minutes ticked inexorably by on the church clock. An apprehensive feeling descended on us: he was half an hour ... three quarters of an hour ... an hour late! And then – as I realize all the more clearly every day – then came the tragedy of my life. He turned up.

I'm a professional failure. No one has ever tried to buy my silence. That proves it.

I can't stay long, but I needed to take refuge for a moment. The Devil is everywhere, seeking whom he may devour ...

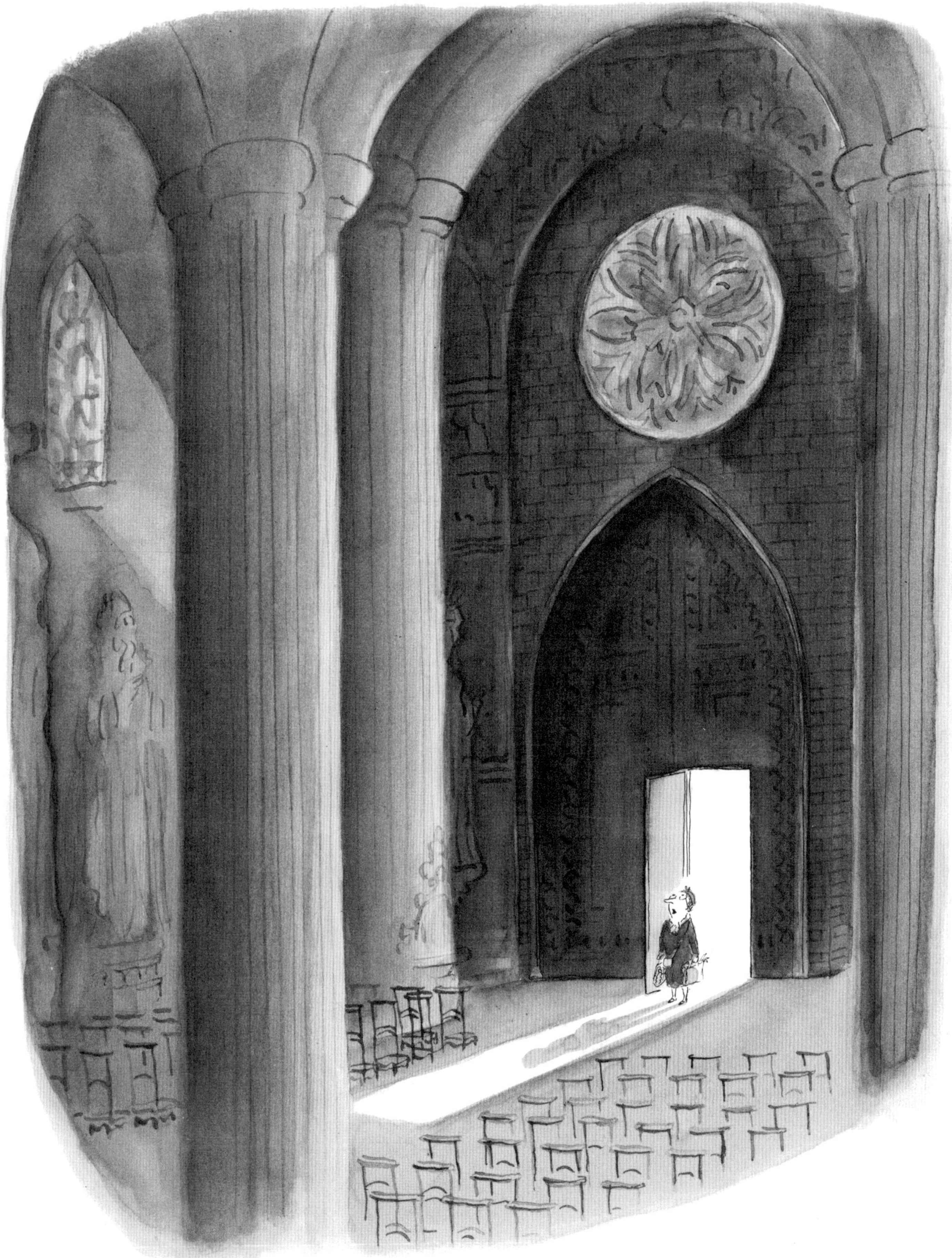

*I'm looking for people in whom I detect such potential for gratitude that I can help them to **benefit** from my deep desire to do good.*

*I'm on the point of being Born Again, but I'd be glad if you wouldn't mention it during dinner. It might be **premature**.*

It happens in two stages. First I tell myself, "I have my memories. They're mine and no one can take them away from me." And then I wonder, "Who'd want them anyway?"

I was watching the big match last night. Paris-Saint-Germain against Marseille. I don't know what came over me, but I imagined one team, Paris-Saint-Germain, represented the women who'd wanted me, and the other, Marseille, represented the women who hadn't. Marseille crushed Paris-Saint-Germain. It was a severe blow, and what's more, this morning I have a guilty conscience about the P.S.G. supporters.

Charles! How long have you been here?

So you see, young Gilbert, it's thanks to the touch of deep despair in my glance (and I can assure you I have cultivated it carefully) that I have aroused such fervent hopes in many a feminine breast.

You do get childish behaviour, of course. A few years ago the secretaries decided to vote for the dishiest man in the office. When Yvonne retired, she told me that I had in fact been the winner, but I was set aside in favour of Machart, head of personnel. Only a little incident, yes, but it does cast an interesting light on the way the wheels of power go round.

Well, if Love turned up again, I'd reply: All present and correct!

And then I said: "You want me? Very well, you shall have me!"

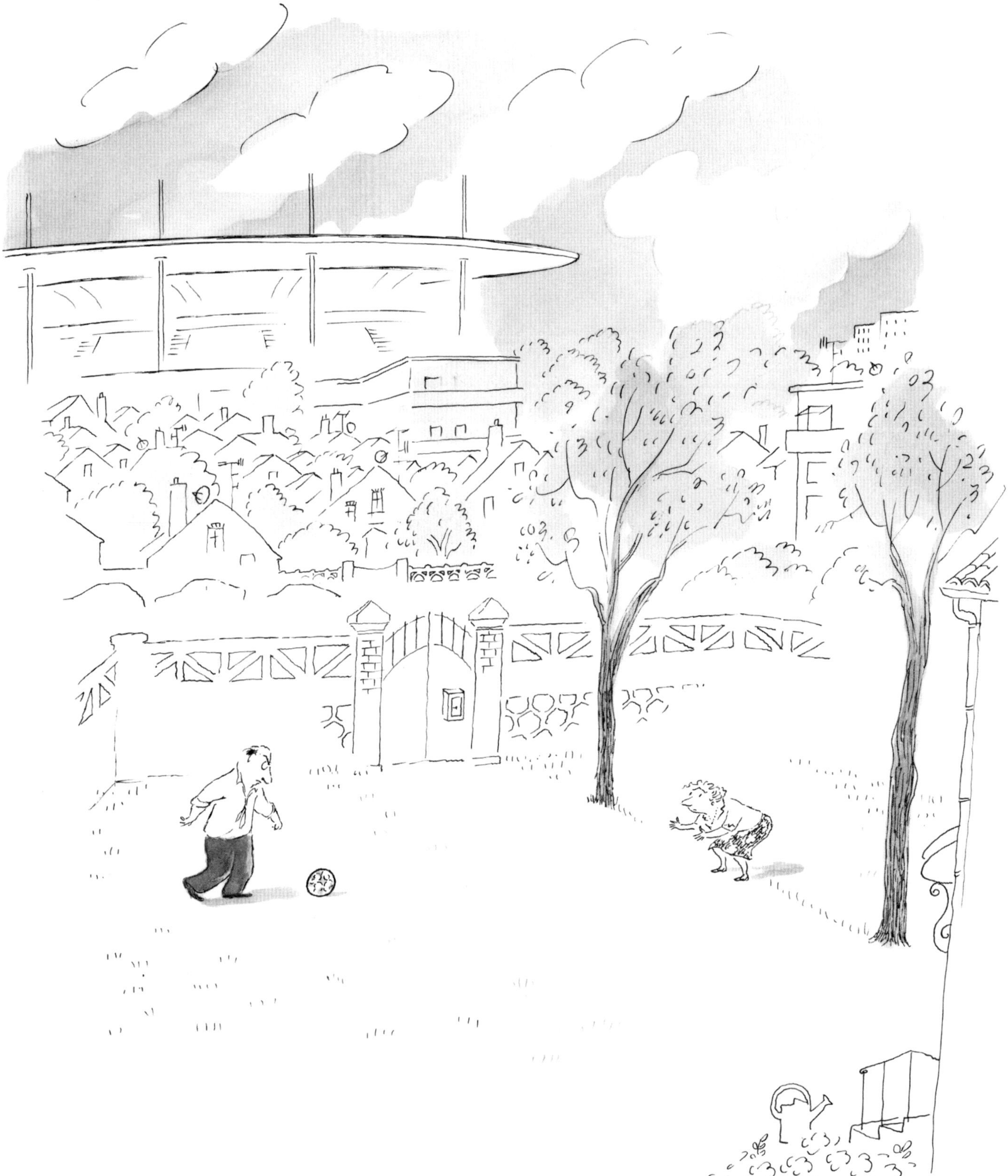

It's as much your job as mine to go and ring that bell!

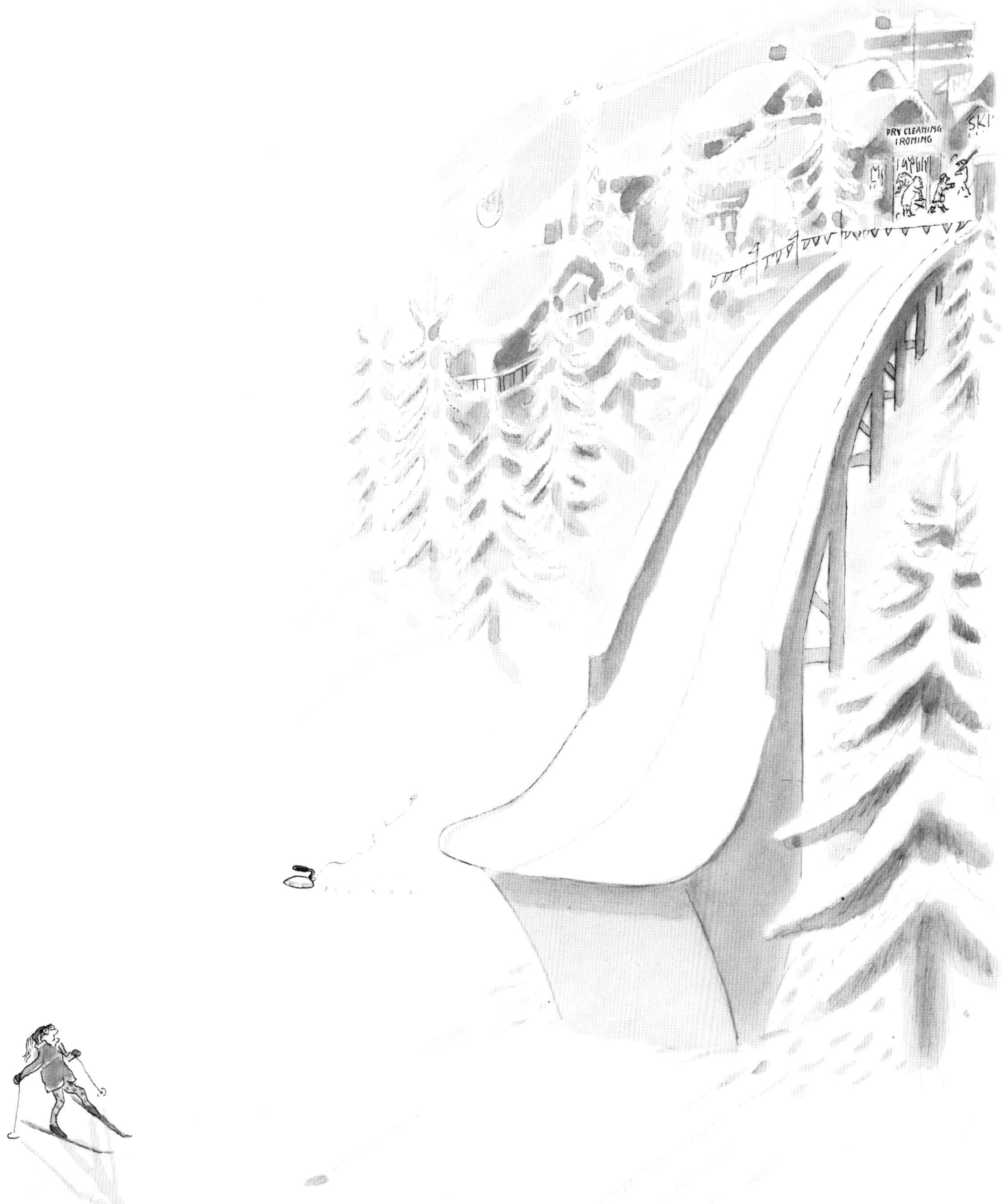
DRY CLEANING
IRONING

If I get to be a hundred years old they'll put me on the telly, and I'll give totally phoney advice about how to live that long.

After five years of research, your wife Nora proves that Pterodactylus erectus became extinct nine hundred thousand years ago. Nora is young (well, twenty years younger than you), and her success annoys you. You do the calculations again, but in your haste you're a hundred thousand years out. Professor Carrington, who has been chasing Nora for months, leaps to her defence and, on the pretext of work, carries her off to the Meteor Hotel. Two days later, a prey to remorse, she returns. And now, for a mistake lasting just two days, whereas yours was a mistake of a hundred thousand years, you propose to write off nine years of life together!

It works!

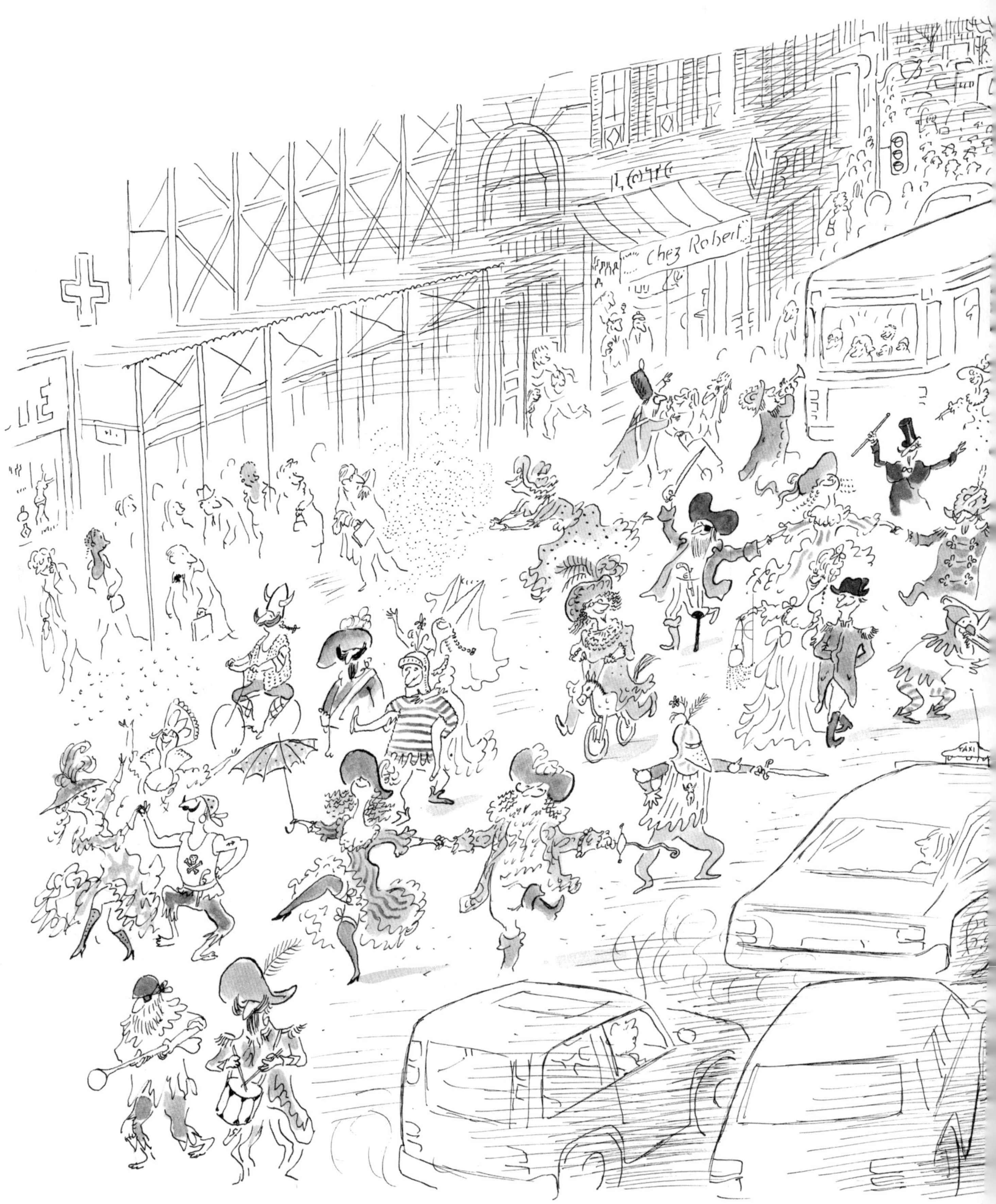
Chez Robert
TAXI

It makes me feel like reading history books.

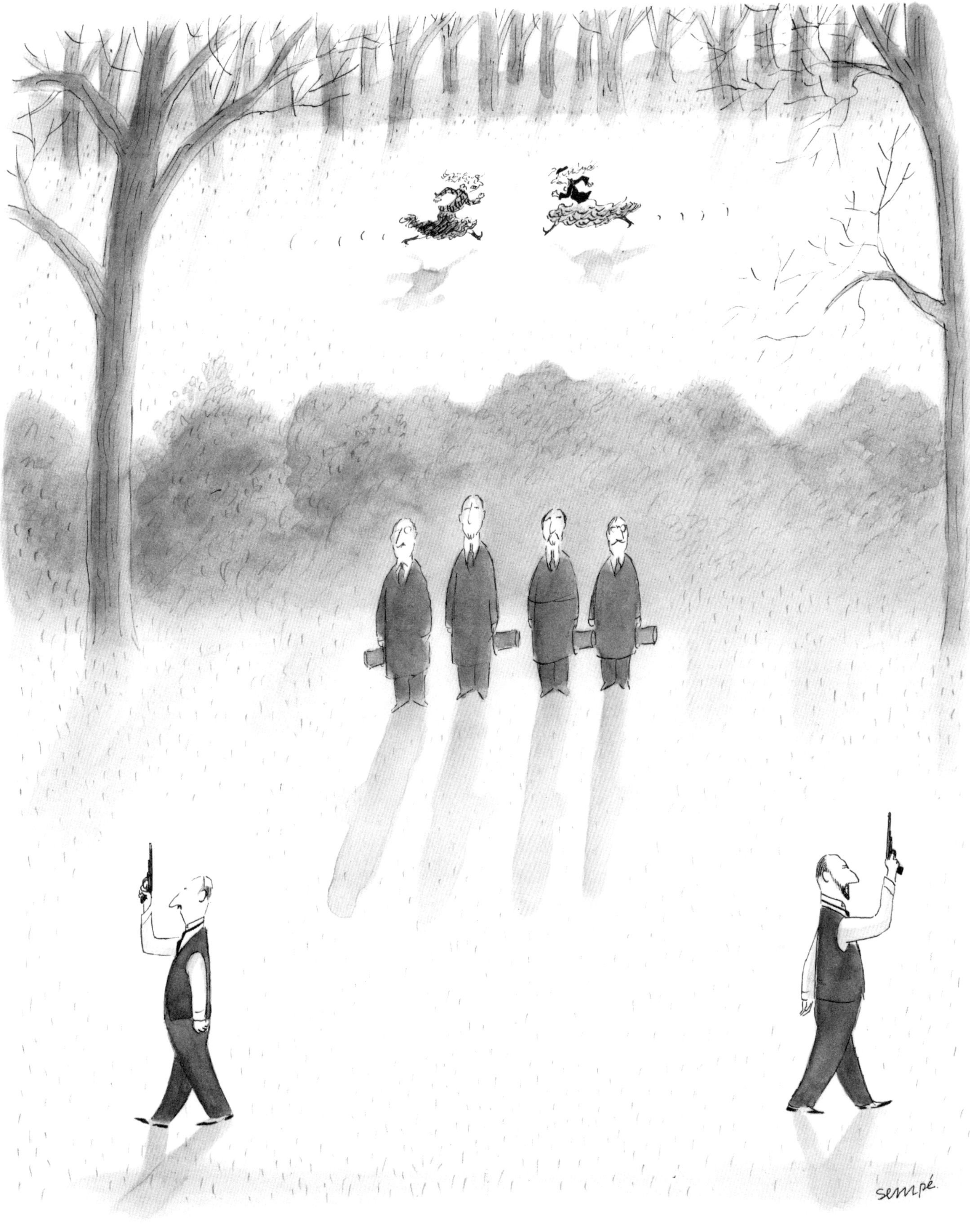
sempé.

Lots of people have wanted to buy that clock, but I've never been able to get it down.

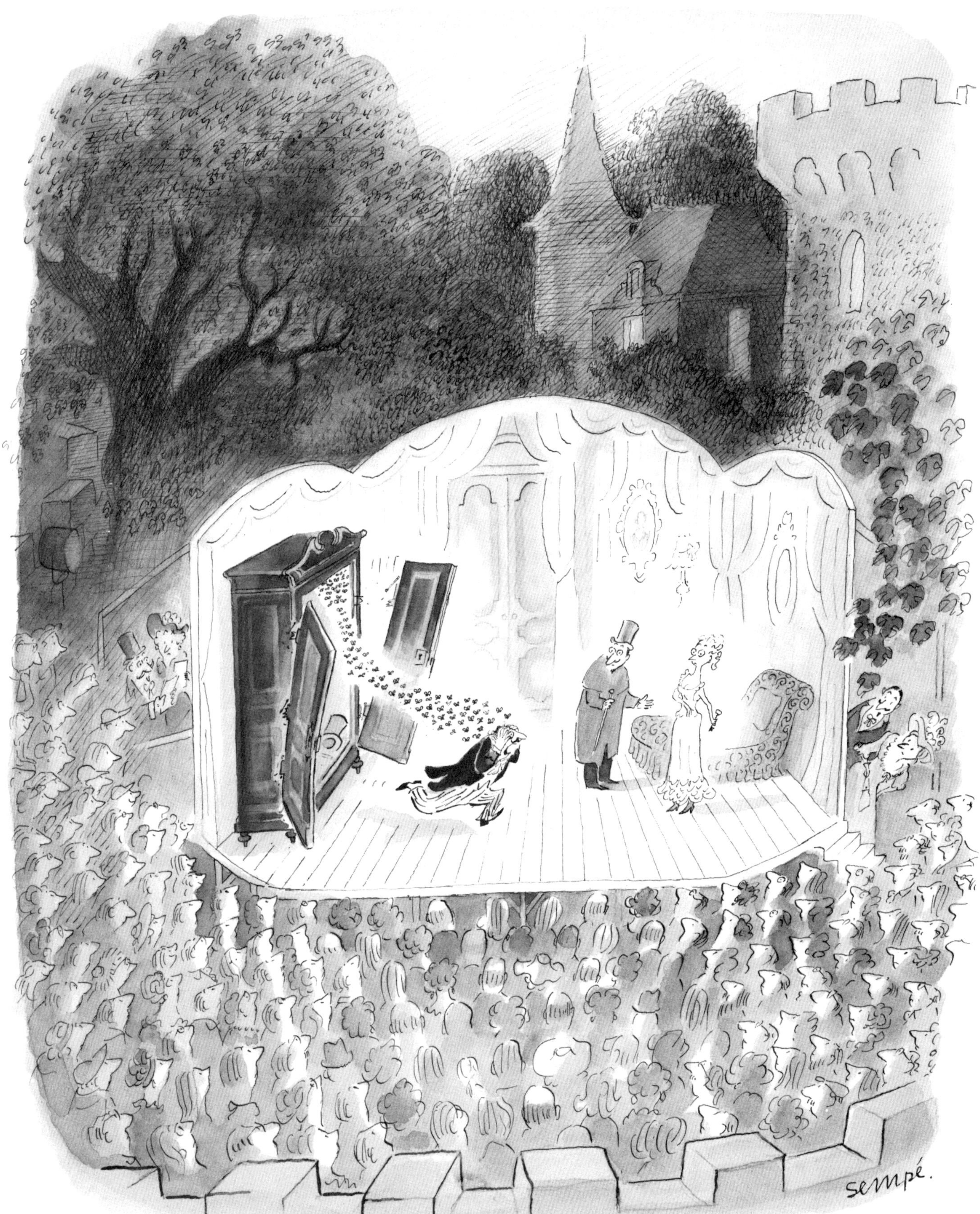
Sempé.

*It took millions of years for what is now known as the human race to rise from the watery element.
So it's odd that we're so irresistibly tempted to get back into it.*

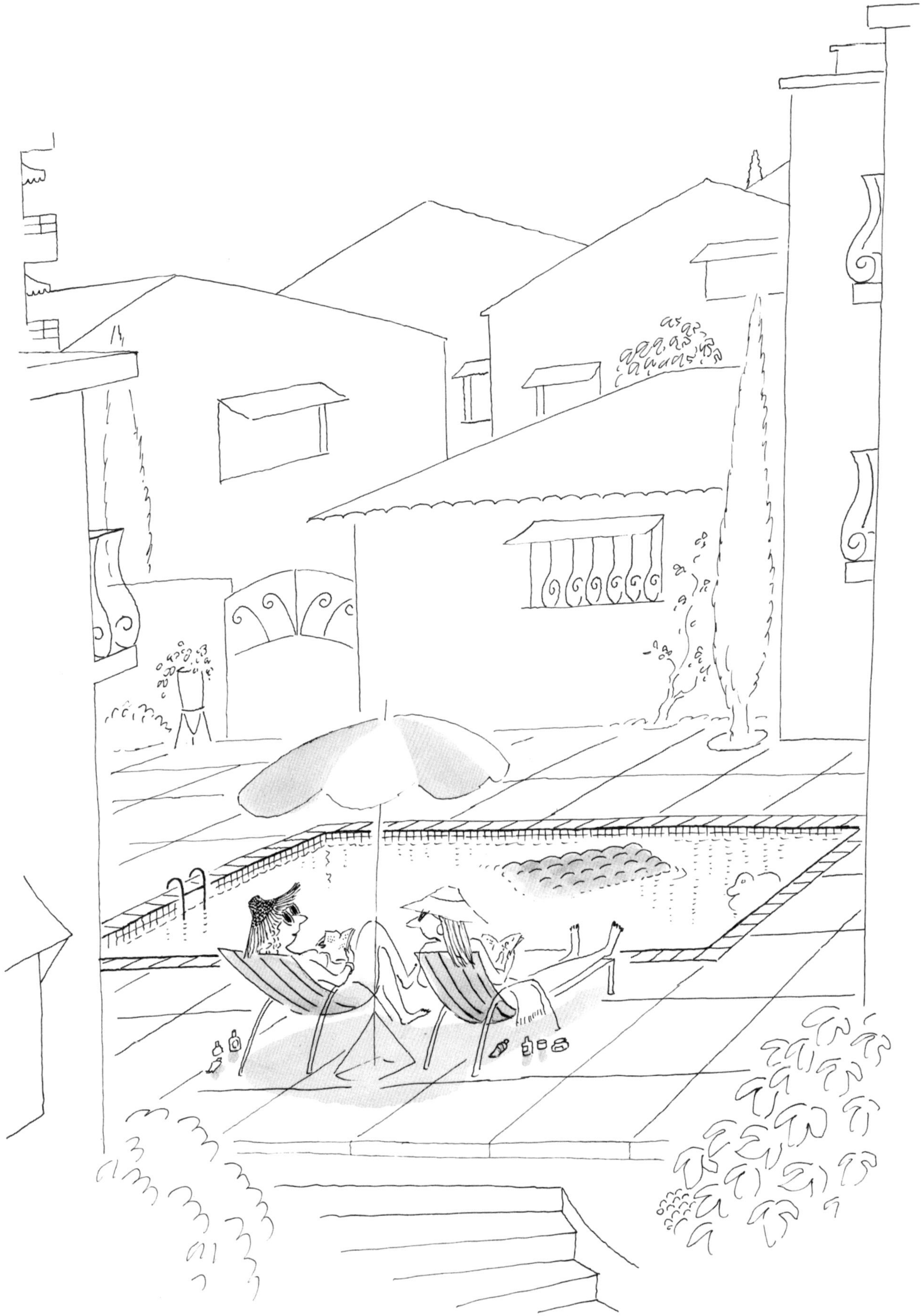

A delightful family Sunday together. Our children, their friends, our grandchildren. General conversation about life, its difficulties, its hopes and fears, the youth of today. "What should we do about the young, how can we help them?" A discussion which turned gradually into: "What should we do about the old?"

Delicious lunch, took rather a long time. His breadth of culture may appear impressive, but frankly I can find all his anecdotes and quotations on the Internet within five minutes.

When we consider the gaiety and merriment so characteristic of your work, communicating the joyful mood so sorely needed these days, should we not also ask whether, at the end of the day, it does not arise from deep-seated egotism and total indifference to the misfortunes of others?

Listen, we'd better take a break from seeing each other. You and I are so superbly well informed that the briefest of conversations leaves us utterly exhausted.

I only get two hours of lucidity a day.

Phaidon Press Limited
Regent's Wharf
All Saints Street
London N1 9PA

Phaidon Press Inc.
180 Varick Street
New York, NY 10014

www.phaidon.com

English Edition © 2006 Phaidon Press Ltd
First published in French as
Beau Temps by Éditions Denoël
© 1999 Sempé and Éditions Denoël

ISBN 0 7148 4544 2

A CIP catalogue record for this book is
available from the British Library.

All rights reserved. No part of this
publication may be reproduced, stored in a
retrieval system or transmitted, in any form,
or by any means, electronic, mechanical,
photocopying, recording or otherwise,
without the written permission of
Phaidon Press Limited.

Translated by Anthea Bell
Designed by James Cartledge and
Phil Cleaver of etal-design
Printed in China